For Edite, with love

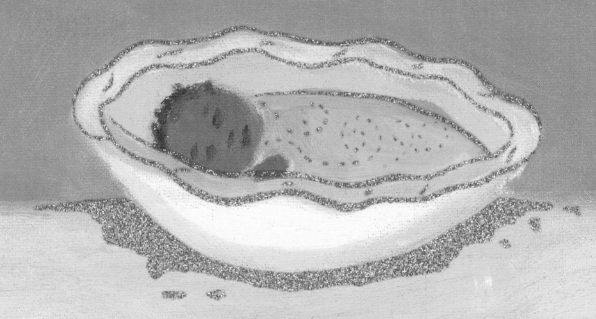

http://www.randomhouse.com/

Library of Congress Cataloging-in-Publication Data
Spohn, Kate. The mermaids' lullaby / by Kate Spohn.   p.   cm.
Summary: Mer-mommies and mer-daddies put their babies to sleep beneath the sea.
ISBN 0-679-89175-7 (trade). — ISBN 0-679-99175-1 (lib. bdg.)
[1. Mermaids—Fiction. 2. Babies—Fiction.] I. Title. PZ7.S7636So 1998 [E]—dc21 97-39770

Manufactured in China   10 9 8 7 6 5 4 3 2 1

The Mermaids' Lullaby

by Kate Spohn

Sleepy, sleepy mermaid babies,
time to tuck beneath seaweed sheets.

Let your bright eyes shut
as your sweet shell ears hear an ocean song.

Listen to the fiddling of the crabs,

the tap-tapping of the sea urchins,

the flashing of the fish,

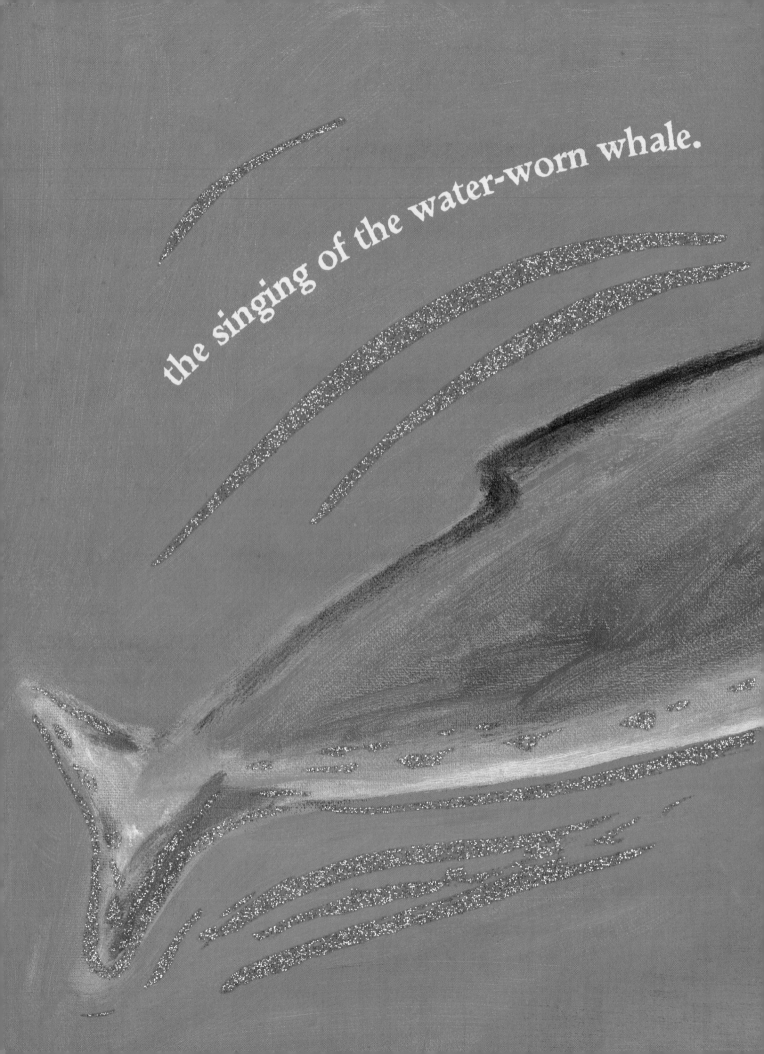

the singing of the water-worn whale.

Sleepy, sleepy mermaid babies,

time to hold mermaid dolls

in your tiny starfish hands.

Listen to the bubbly voices

of mer-mommies and daddies

as they hang found-lost treasures

in the ocean-washed ballroom

and sweep shell shapes into the sandy floor.

Feel the wave of music
as the celebration swells

and let the soft, salty sea rock, rock you

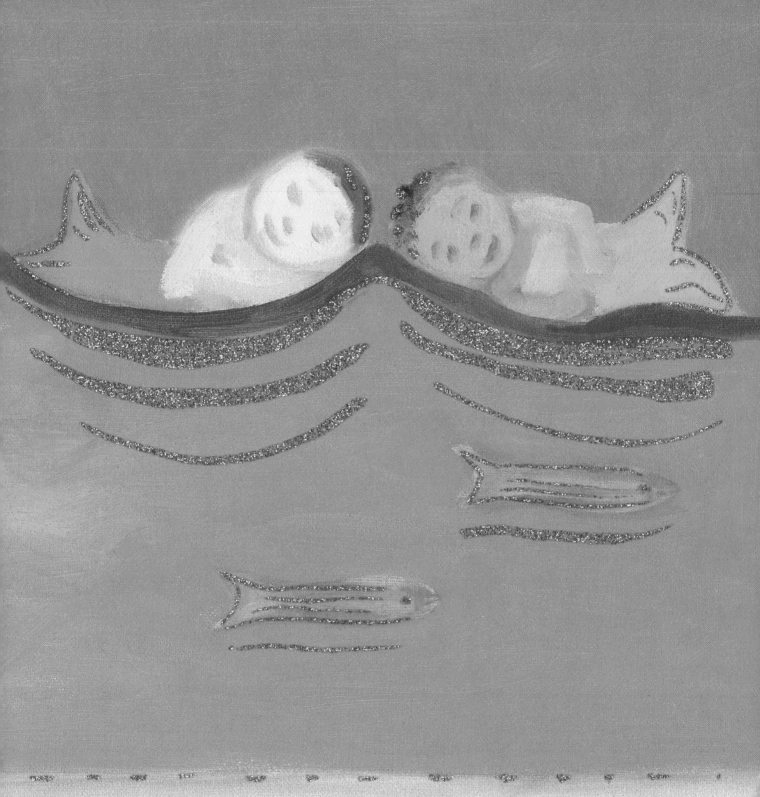

as the mermaids dance you

deep into your dreams . . .